BLACK BEAUTY

Coloring Book

Anna Sewell

Illustrated by
JOHN GREEN

DOVER PUBLICATIONS, INC.

MINEOLA, NEW YORK

Bibliographical Note

Black Beauty Coloring Book is a new work, first published by Dover Publications, Inc., in 1996. The new abridgment of the story is by Candace Ward.

International Standard Book Number: 0-486-29272-X

Manufactured in the United States of America
Dover Publications, Inc., 31 East 2nd Street, Mineola, N.Y. 11501

THE FIRST PLACE that I can well remember was a large pleasant meadow with a pond of clear water in it. Some shady trees leaned over it, rushes and water-lilies grew at the deep end. Over the hedge on one side we looked into a plowed field, and on the other we looked over a gate at our master's house. There were six young colts in the meadow besides me; they were older than I was. We used to gallop all together round and round the field, as hard as we could go. Sometimes we had rather rough play, for they would frequently bite and kick as well as gallop.

One day, when there was a good deal of kicking, my mother whinnied to me to come to her, and then she said: "I wish you to pay attention to what I am going to say to you. The colts who live here are very good colts, but they are cart-horse colts, and, of course, they have not learned manners. You have been well bred and well born; your father has a great name in these parts, and your grandfather won the cup two years at the Newmarket races; your grandmother had the sweetest temper of any horse I ever knew, and I think you have never seen me kick or bite. I hope you will grow up gentle and good, and never learn bad ways; do your work with a good will, lift your feet up well when you trot, and never bite or kick even in play." I have never forgotten my mother's advice.

One day in the early spring, before I was two years old, I and the other colts were feeding at the lower part of the field. Suddenly we heard what sounded like the cry of dogs. The oldest of the colts raised his head, pricked his ears, and said, "There are the hounds!" and immediately cantered off followed by the rest of us to the upper part of the field, where we could look over the hedge and see several fields beyond. My mother and an old riding horse of our master's were also standing near.

"They have found a hare," said my mother, "and if they come this way we shall see the hunt."

And soon the dogs were all tearing down the field next to ours. After them came a number of men on horseback, all galloping as fast as they could. They were soon away into the fields lower down; here it seemed as if they had come to a stand; the dogs left off barking, and ran about with their noses to the ground.

"They have lost the scent," said the old horse, "perhaps the hare will get off."

"What hare?" I said.

"Oh! I don't know *what* hare; any hare they can find will do for the dogs and men to run after." Before long the dogs began a "yo! yo, o, o!" and back they came all together at full speed.

Just then a hare wild with fright rushed by. On came the dogs; they burst over the bank, leapt the stream, and came dashing across the field, followed by the huntsmen. The hare tried to get through the fence; it was too thick, and she turned sharp round to make for

the road, but it was too late; the dogs were upon her with their wild cries; we heard one shriek, and that was the end of her.

As for me, I was so astonished that I did not at first see what was going on by the brook; but when I did look, there was a sad sight; two fine horses were down, one was struggling in the stream, and the other was groaning on the grass. One of the riders was getting out of the water covered with mud, the other lay quite still.

Many of the riders had gone to the young man; but my master was the first to raise him. His head fell back and his arms hung down, and everyone looked very serious. They carried the young man to our master's house. I heard afterwards that it was young George Gordon, the squire's only son.

When Mr. Bond, the farrier, came to look at the black horse that lay groaning on the grass, he felt him all over, and shook his head; one of his legs was broken. Then someone ran to our master's house and came back with a gun; presently there was a loud bang and a dreadful shriek, and then all was still; the black horse moved no more.

My mother seemed much troubled; she said she had known that horse for years, and that his name was Rob Roy; he was a good bold horse, and there was no vice in him. She would never go to that part of the field afterwards.

Not many days after, we heard the church bell tolling for a long time; and looking over the gate we saw a long strange black coach covered with black cloth and drawn by two black horses; after that came another and another, and all were black, while the bell kept tolling, tolling. They were carrying young Gordon to the church-yard to bury him. What they did with Rob Roy I never knew; but 'twas all for one little hare.

I was now beginning to grow handsome; my coat had grown fine and soft, and was bright black. I had one white foot, and a pretty white star on my forehead.

When I was four years old, Squire Gordon came to look at me. He examined my eyes, my mouth, and my legs; and then I had to walk and trot and gallop before him. My master said he would break me in himself, and he lost no time about it, for the next day he began.

After I had learned to wear the bit and bridle and to carry my master, it was time to break me to harness. My master often drove me in double harness with my mother, because she was steady, and could teach me how to go better than a strange horse. She told me

the better I behaved, the better I should be treated, and that it was wisest always to do my best to please my master. "But," said she, "there are a great many kinds of men; I hope you will fall into good hands; but a horse never knows who may buy him, or who may drive him; it is all a chance for us, but still I say, do your best, wherever it is, and keep up your good name."

Early in May there came a man from Squire Gordon's, who took me away to the Hall, and so I left my first home. At Squire Gordon's, the groom led me to the stables, fed me some oats, and then left. The next day I was brought up for my master. I found he was a very good rider, and thoughtful for his horse too. When he came home his lady was at the hall door as he rode up.

"Well, my dear," she said, "how do you like him?"

"He is exactly what I expected," he replied; "a pleasanter creature I never wished to mount. What shall we call him?"

She said, "He is really quite a beauty—what do you say to calling him Black Beauty?"

"Black Beauty—why, yes, I think that is a very good name. If you like it shall be his name," and so it was.

When John, the Squire's coachman, went into the stable, he told the stableboy James that master and mistress had chosen a good sensible name for me. James said, "If it was not for bringing back the past, I should have named him Rob Roy, for I never saw two horses more alike."

"That's no wonder," said John, "didn't you know that Farmer Grey's old Duchess was the mother of both of them?"

I had never heard of that before, and so poor Rob Roy who was killed at that hunt was my brother! I did not wonder that my mother was so troubled.

One day late in the autumn, my master had a long journey to go on business. I was put into the dog-cart, and John went with his master. There had been a great deal of rain, and now the wind was very high. We went along merrily till we came to the toll-bar and the low wooden bridge. The man at the gate said the river was rising fast, and he feared it would be a bad night.

At the town, the master's business engaged him a long time, and we did not start for home till rather late in the afternoon. The wind was then much higher, and I heard the master say to John, he had never been out in such a storm.

"I wish we were well out of this wood," said my master.

"Yes, sir," said John, "it would be rather awkward if one of these branches came down upon us."

The words were scarcely out of his mouth, when crashing down among the other trees came an oak, right across the road before us. I stopped still, and I believe I trembled; of course, I did not turn round or run away.

"That was a very near touch," said my master. "What's to be done now?"

"Well, sir, we can't drive over that tree nor yet get round it; there will be nothing for it but to go back to the four cross-ways, and that will be a good six miles before we get round to the bridge again; we will be late, but the horse is fresh."

By the time we got to the bridge it was very nearly dark, and we could just see that the water was over the middle of it; but as that happened sometimes when the floods were out, master did not stop. The moment my feet touched the first part of the bridge, I felt sure there was something wrong. I dare not go forward, and I made a dead stop. "Go on, Beauty," said my master, and he gave me a touch with the whip, but I dare not stir; he gave me a sharp cut, I jumped, but I dare not go forward.

"There's something wrong, sir," said John, and he sprang out of the cart and came to my head and looked all about. He tried to lead me forward. "Come on, Beauty, what's the matter?"

Just then the man at the toll-gate on the other side ran out of the house, tossing a torch about like one mad.

"Hoy, hoy, hoy, halloo, stop!" he cried.

"What's the matter?" shouted my master.

"The bridge is broken in the middle and part of it is carried away; if you come on you'll be into the river."

"Thank God!" said my master. "You Beauty!" said John and took the bridle and gently turned me round to the right-hand road by the river side. I trotted quietly along, the wheels hardly making a sound on the soft road.

At last we arrived at the house, and saw a light at the hall door and at the upper windows. As we came up mistress ran out saying, "Oh! I have been so anxious, fancying all sorts of things. Have you had no accident?"

"No, my dear; but if your Black Beauty had not been wiser than we were, we should all have been carried down the river." I heard no more, as they went into the house, and John took me to the stable. Oh! what a good supper he gave me that night, and such a thick bed of straw, and I was glad of it, for I was tired.

Not long after this, it was decided by my master and mistress to pay a visit to some friends who lived about forty-six miles from our home, and James was to drive them. The first day we travelled thirty-two miles. When we reached the town where we were to spend the night, we stopped at the principal hotel. Two ostlers came to take us out. The head ostler, a pleasant, active little man, led me to a long stable, with six or eight stalls in it, and two or three horses. The other man brought Ginger, Squire Gordon's other horse; James stood by while we were rubbed down.

Later on in the evening, a traveller's horse was brought in by the second ostler, and whilst he was cleaning him, a young man with a pipe in his mouth lounged into the stable to gossip.

"I say, Towler," said the ostler, "just run up the ladder into the loft and put some hay down into this horse's rack, will you? only lay down your pipe."

"All right," said the other, and went up through the trap door; soon James came in to look at us the last thing, and then the door was locked.

I cannot say how long I had slept, nor what time in the night it was, but I woke up very uncomfortable. The air seemed all thick and choking; the stable was full of smoke, and I hardly knew how to breathe. The other horses were all awake; some were pulling at their halters, others were stamping.

At last I heard steps outside, and the ostler who had put up the traveller's horse burst into the stable, and began to untie the horses, and try to lead them out. The first horse would not go with him. He tried the second and third; they too would not stir. He tried us all by turns and then left the stable.

No doubt we were very foolish, but danger seemed to be all round, and there was nobody we knew to trust in, and all was strange and uncertain. Then I heard a cry of "Fire" outside, and the old ostler quietly and quickly came in; he got one horse out, and went to another. The next thing I heard was James's voice: "Come, Beauty, on with your bridle, my boy; we'll soon be out of this." He took the scarf off his neck, and tied it lightly over my eyes, and patting and coaxing he led me out of the stable.

A man stepped forward and took me, and James darted back into the stable. I kept my eye fixed on the stable door, where the smoke poured out thicker than ever, and I could see flashes of red light; presently I heard above all the stir and din a loud clear voice, which I knew was master's: "James Howard! James Howard! are you there?" There was no answer, but the next moment I saw James coming through the smoke leading Ginger with him; she was coughing violently, and he was not able to speak.

"My brave lad!" said master, "when you have got your breath, James, we'll get out of this place as quickly as we can."

The next morning the master came to see how we were and to speak to James. I could see that James looked very happy, and I thought the master was proud of him.

Soon afterward, James left us, having secured a position as a groom for our master's brother-in-law. In his place came Joe Green, a local lad of but fourteen and a half years. One night, a few days after James left, I was lying down in my straw fast asleep, when I was suddenly awoke by the stable bell ringing very loud. I heard the door of John's house open, and his feet running up to the Hall. He was back again in no time; he unlocked the stable door, and came in, calling out, "Wake up, Beauty, you must go well now, if ever you did," and almost before I could think, he had got the saddle on my back and the bridle on my head; he just ran round for his coat, and then took me at a quick trot up to the Hall door. The Squire stood there with a lamp in his hand.

"Now, John," he said, "ride for your life, that is, for your mistress's life; there is not a moment to lose; give this note to Doctor White; give your horse a rest at the Inn, and be back as soon as you can."

John said, "Yes, sir," and was on my back in a minute. Away we went through the Park and through the village, and down the hill. There was before us a long piece of level road by the river side; John said to me, "Now, Beauty, do your best," and so I did; I don't believe

that my old grandfather who won the race at Newmarket could have gone faster. The church clock struck three as we drew up at the Doctor's door. John rang the bell twice, and then knocked at the door like thunder. A window was thrown up, and Doctor White put his head out and said, "What do you want?"

"Mrs. Gordon is very ill, sir. Master needs you at once; he thinks she will die if you cannot get there—here is a note."

"Wait," he said, "I will come." He shut the window, and was soon at the door. "The worst of it is," he said, "that my horse has been out all day and is quite done up; my son has just been sent for, and he has taken the other. What is to be done? Can I have your horse?"

"He has come at a gallop nearly all the way, sir, and I was to give him a rest; but I think my master would not be against it if you think fit, sir."

"All right," he said, "I will soon be ready."

I will not tell about our way back; the Doctor was a heavier man than John, and not so good a rider; however, I did my very best, and soon we were in the Park. My master was at the Hall door, for he had heard us coming. He spoke not a word; the Doctor went into the house with him, and Joe led me to the stable. I had not a dry hair on

my body, the water ran down my legs, and I steamed all over. Poor Joe! he did the very best he knew. He rubbed my legs and my chest, but he did not put my warm cloth on me; he thought I was so hot I should not like it. Then he gave me a pail full of water and I drank it all; then he gave me some hay and some corn, and went away. Soon I began to shake and tremble, and turned deadly cold. Oh! how I wished for my warm thick cloth as I stood and trembled. After a long while I heard John at the door; I gave a low moan, for I was now very ill; a strong inflammation had attacked my lungs, and I could not draw my breath without pain. John nursed me night and day and my master often came to see me.

"My poor Beauty," he said one day, "my good horse, you saved your mistress's life, Beauty!" I was very glad to hear that, for it seems the Doctor had said if we had been a little longer it would have been too late. John told my master he never saw a horse go so fast in his life, it seemed as if the horse knew what was the matter. Of course I did, though John thought not; at least I knew as much as this, that John and I must go at the top of our speed, and that it was for the sake of the mistress.

I do not know how long I was ill. The horse doctor came every day. One day he bled me; John held a pail for the blood; I felt very faint after it, and thought I should die, and I believe they all thought so too, but at length I regained my health.

I had not lived in this place three years, but sad changes were about to come over us. Our mistress was ill. The Doctor was often at the house, and the master looked grave and anxious. Then we heard that she must go to a warm country for two or three years. Everybody was sorry; but the master began directly to make arrangements for breaking up his establishment.

The last sad day had come; Ginger and I brought the carriage up to the Hall door for the last time. The servants brought out cushions and rugs and master came down the steps carrying the mistress in his arms; he placed her carefully in the carriage, while the house servants stood round crying. "Good-bye, again," he said, "we shall not forget any of you," and he got in—"Drive on, John."

When we reached the railway station, I think mistress walked from the carriage to the waiting room. As soon as Joe had taken the things out of the carriage, John called him to stand by the horses, while he went on the platform. Poor Joe! he stood close up to our heads to hide his tears. Soon the train came puffing up into the station; then two or three minutes, and the doors were slammed to; the guard whistled and the train glided away, leaving behind it only clouds of white smoke, and some very heavy hearts.

When it was quite out of sight, John came back: "We shall never see her again," he said—"never." He took the reins, mounted the box, and with Joe drove slowly home; but it was not our home now.

The next morning after breakfast John put the saddle on Ginger and the leading rein on me, and rode us across the country about fifteen miles to Earlshall Park, where the Earl of W--- lived. There was a very fine house and a great deal of stabling; we went into the yard through a stone gateway, and John asked for Mr. York, our new coachman. It was some time before he came. He was a fine-looking, middle-aged man, and his voice said at once that he expected to be obeyed.

"Now, Mr. Manly," he said, after carefully looking at us both, "I can see no fault in these horses, but I should like to know if there is anything particular in either of these that you would like to mention."

"Well," said John, "I don't believe there is a better pair of horses in the country, but they are not alike. The black one is the most perfect temper I ever knew; but the chestnut I fancy must have had bad treatment. She came to us snappish and suspicious, but when she found what sort of place ours was, it all went off by degrees; for three years I have never seen the smallest sign of temper, but she is naturally a more irritable constitution than the black horse; and if she were ill-used or unfairly treated, she would not be unlikely to give tit for tat; you know that many high-mettled horses will do so."

They were going out of the stable when John stopped and said, "I had better mention that we have never used the 'bearing rein' with either of them; the black horse never had one on."

"Well," said York, "if they come here they must wear the bearing rein. I prefer a loose rein myself, and his lordship is always very reasonable about horses; but my lady—that's another thing—she will have style; and if her carriage horses are not reined up tight, she wouldn't look at them. I always stand out against the gag-bit, but it must be tight up when my lady rides!"

"I am sorry for it, very sorry," said John, "but I must go now, or I shall lose the train."

The next day Lord W--- came to look at us; he seemed pleased with our appearance. "I have great confidence in these horses," he said, "from the character my friend Mr. Gordon has given me of them." York then told him what John had said about us.

"Well," said he, "you must keep an eye on the mare, and put the bearing rein easy; I dare say they will do very well with a little humouring at first."

In the afternoon we were harnessed and put in the carriage, and led round to the front of the house. It was all very grand, and three or four times as large as the old house at Birtwick, but not half so pleasant. Presently we heard the rustling sound of silk as my lady came down the flight of stone steps. She stepped around to look at us; she was a tall, proud-looking woman, and did not seemed pleased about something, but she said nothing, and got into the carriage. This was the first time of wearing a bearing rein, and though it certainly was a nuisance not to be able to get my head down now and then, it did not pull my head higher than I was accustomed to carry it. I felt anxious about Ginger, but she seemed quiet and content.

The next day we were again at the door; we heard the silk dress rustle, and the lady come down the steps, and in an imperious voice she said, "York, you must put those horses' heads higher; they are not fit to be seen."

York got down and said very respectfully, "I beg your pardon, my lady, but these horses have not been reined up for three years, and my lord said it would be safer to bring them to it by degrees; but if your ladyship pleases, I can take them up a little more."

"Do so," she said.

Day by day, hole by hole, our bearing reins were shortened, and instead of looking forward with pleasure to having my harness put on as I used to do, I began to dread it. Ginger too seemed restless, though she said very little.

One day my lady came down later than usual, and the silk rustled more than ever. "Drive to the Duchess of B---'s," she said, and then after a pause, "Are you never going to get those horses' heads up, York? Raise them at once."

York came to me first. He drew my head back and fixed the rein so tight that it was almost intolerable; then he went to Ginger. She had a good idea of what was coming, and the moment York took the rein in order to shorten it, she took her opportunity and reared up so suddenly that York had his nose roughly hit, and his hat knocked off; the groom was nearly thrown off his legs. At once they both flew to her head, but she was a match for them, and went on plunging, rearing, and kicking in a most desperate manner; at last she kicked right over the carriagepole and fell down, after giving me a severe blow on my near quarter. York promptly sat himself down flat on her head to prevent her struggling, at the same time calling out, "Unbuckle the black horse!" The groom soon set me free from Ginger and the carriage and led me to my box.

Before long, Ginger was led in by two grooms, a good deal knocked about and bruised. York came with her and gave his orders, and then came to look at me. He felt me all over, and soon found the place above my hock where I had been kicked. It was swelled and painful; he ordered it to be sponged with hot water, and then some lotion was put on.

Ginger was never put into the carriage again but when she was well of her bruises, one of Lord W---'s younger sons, Lord George, said he should like to have her; he was sure she would make a good hunter. As for me, I was obliged still to go in the carriage, and had a fresh partner called Max; he had always been used to the tight rein.

What I suffered with that rein for four long months in my lady's carriage, it would be hard to describe; but I am quite sure that, had it lasted much longer, either my health or my temper would have given way. Before that, I never knew what it was to foam at the mouth, but now the action of the sharp bit on my tongue and jaw,

and the constrained position of my head and throat always caused me to froth at the mouth more or less. I was well treated in many ways, but nothing was ever done to relieve me of the bearing rein.

Early in the spring, Lord W--- and part of his family went up to London, and took York with them. I and Ginger and some other horses were left at home for use, and the head groom was left in charge.

The Lady Harriet, who was a great invalid, never went out in the carriage, and the Lady Anne preferred riding on horseback with her brother, or cousins. She was a perfect horsewoman, and as gay and gentle as she was beautiful. She chose me for her horse, and named me Black Auster. I enjoyed these rides very much in the clear cold air, sometimes with Ginger, sometimes with Lizzie, a bright bay mare.

There was a gentleman of the name of Blantyre staying at the Hall; he always rode Lizzie, and praised her so much that one day Lady Anne ordered the side-saddle to be put on her, and the other saddle on me. When we came to the door, the gentleman seemed very uneasy. "How is this?" he said, "Are you tired of your good Black Auster?"

"Oh! no, not at all," she replied, "but I am amiable enough to let you ride him for once and I will try your charming Lizzie. You must confess she is far more like a lady's horse than my own favorite."

"Do let me advise you not to mount her," he said. "She is a charming creature, but she is too nervous for a lady."

"My dear cousin," said Lady Anne, laughing, "pray do not trouble your good careful head about me; I have been a horsewoman ever since I was a baby, and I have followed the hounds a great many times. I intend to try this Lizzie, so please help me to mount."

There was no more to be said. Just as we were moving off, a servant came out with a slip of paper and message from the Lady Harriet—"Would they ask this question for her at Dr. Ashley's, and bring the answer?"

We went along gaily enough till we came to the Doctor's house. Blantyre alighted at the gate, and was going to open it for Lady Anne, but she said, "I will wait for you here, and you can hang Auster's rein on the gate." He looked at her doubtfully—"I will not be five minutes," he said.

"Oh, do not hurry. Lizzie and I shall not run away."

He hung my rein on one of the iron spikes, and was soon hidden among the trees. Lizzie was standing quietly by the side of the road a few paces off with her back to me. My young mistress was sitting easily with a loose rein, humming a little song. Just then some cart horses and several young colts came trotting along in a very disorderly manner, while a boy behind was cracking a great whip. The colts were wild and frolicsome, and one of them bolted across the road, and blundered up against Lizzie's hind legs; she gave a violent kick, and dashed off into a headlong gallop. It was so sudden that Lady Anne was nearly unseated, but she soon recovered herself. Blantyre came running to the gate; he looked anxiously about, and just caught sight of the flying figure, now far away on the

road. In an instant he sprang into the saddle, and giving me a free rein, we dashed after them, trying to keep Lady Anne in sight as she and Lizzie flew around the bends of the road.

After a long chase, we caught sight of her green habit flying on before us. My lady's hat was gone, and her long brown hair was streaming behind her. It was clear that the roughness of the ground had very much lessened Lizzie's speed, and there seemed a chance that we might overtake her.

About halfway across the heath there had been a wide dyke recently cut, and the earth from the cutting was cast up roughly on the other side. With scarcely a pause Lizzie took the leap, stumbled among the rough clods, and fell. Blantyre gave me a steady rein. I gathered myself well together, and with one determined leap cleared both dyke and bank.

Motionless among the heather, with her face to the earth, lay my poor young mistress. Blantyre kneeled down and called her name— there was no sound; gently he turned her face upward, it was ghastly white, and the eyes were closed. He unbuttoned her habit, loosened her collar, felt her hands and wrists, then started up and looked wildly round him for help.

At no great distance there were two men cutting turf; Blantyre's halloo soon brought them to the spot. The foremost man asked what he could do.

"Can you ride?"

"Well, sir, I bean't much of a horseman, but I can try."

"Then mount this horse, my friend, and ride to the Doctor's and ask him to come instantly—then on to the Hall—bid them send the carriage with Lady Anne's maid and help. I shall stay here."

"All right, sir, I'll do my best." He then somehow scrambled into the saddle, and with a "Gee-up" and a clap on my sides with both his legs, he started on his journey. There was a great deal of hurry and excitement at the Hall after the news became known. I was just turned into my box, and a cloth thrown over me. Ginger was saddled and sent off in great haste for Lord George, and I soon heard the carriage roll out of the yard. It seemed a long time before Ginger came back and before we were left alone; and then she told me that Lady Anne was not dead, but that she had not yet spoken.

Two days after the accident, Blantyre paid me a visit; he patted me and praised me very much, and told Lord George that he was sure the horse knew of Annie's danger as well as he did. I found by their conversation that my young mistress was now out of danger, and would soon be able to ride again.

Reuben Smith was left in charge of the stables when York went to London. No one more thoroughly understood his business than he did, but he had one great fault: the love of drink.

One day it was arranged that Smith should drive Colonel Blantyre to the town in the light brougham, and then ride back; for this purpose, he took the saddle with him, and I was chosen for the journey. After leaving Colonel Blantyre, we left the carriage at the maker's, and Smith rode me to the White Lion. He ordered the ostler to feed me well and have me ready for him at four o'clock. A nail in one of my front shoes had started as I came along, but the ostler did not notice it till just about four o'clock. Smith did not come into the yard till five, and then he said he should not leave till six, as he had met with some old friends. The man then told him of the nail, and asked if he should have the shoe looked to.

"No," said Smith, "that will be all right till we get home." He spoke in a very loud off-hand way, and I thought it very unlike him, not to see about loose nails in our shoes. It was nearly nine o'clock before he called for me, and then it was in a loud rough voice. He seemed in a very bad temper, and almost before he was out of the town he began to gallop, frequently giving me a sharp cut with his whip, though I was going at full speed. The moon had not yet risen, and it was very dark. The roads were stony and going over them at this pace my shoe became looser; when we were near the turnpike gate it came off.

Beyond the turnpike was a long piece of road, upon which fresh stones had just been laid; large sharp stones, over which no horse could be driven quickly without risk of danger. Over this road, with one shoe gone, I was forced to gallop at my utmost speed. Of course my shoeless foot suffered dreadfully; the hoof was broken and split down to the very quick, and the inside was terribly cut by the sharpness of the stones.

This could not go on; the pain was too great. I stumbled, and fell with violence on both my knees. Smith was flung off by my fall, and

owing to the speed I was going at, he must have fallen with great force. I soon recovered my feet and limped to the side of the road. The moon had just risen, and by its light I could see Smith lying a few yards beyond me. He did not rise. I uttered no sound, but I stood there and listened.

It must have been nearly midnight when I heard at a distance the sound of a horse's feet; I was almost sure I could distinguish Ginger's step. I neighed loudly, and was overjoyed to hear an answering neigh from Ginger, and men's voices. They came slowly over the stones, and stopped at the dark figure that lay upon the ground. One of the men jumped out, and stooped down over it. "It is Reuben!" he said.

The other man followed and bent over him. "He's dead," he said; "feel how cold his hands are."

They raised him up, but there was no life, and his hair was soaked with blood. They laid him down again, and came and looked at me. They soon saw my cut knees.

"Why, the horse has been down and thrown him! Who would have thought the black horse would have done that? Nobody thought he could fall."

Robert then attempted to lead me forward. I made a step, but almost fell again. "Hallo! he's bad in his foot as well as his knees; look here—his hoof is cut all to pieces; he might well come down, poor fellow! I tell you what, Ned, I'm afraid it hasn't been all right with Reuben! Just think of him riding a horse over these stones without a shoe!"

The next day, after the farrier had examined my wounds, he said he hoped the joint was not injured, and if so, I should not be spoiled for work, but I should never lose the blemish. I believe they did the best to make a good cure, but it was a long and painful one.

One day, the Earl came into the meadow where I'd been resting, and York was with him. They examined me carefully. The Earl seemed much annoyed. The fall had spoiled the way my knees

looked, and although my health was now mended the Earl decided I must be sold.

About a week after this, I was bought by the master of some livery stables in Bath. Although these stables were not so pleasant and clean as I was used to, I was well fed and cleaned. But in this place I was to get my experience of all the different kinds of bad and ignorant driving to which we horses are subjected.

One morning I was hired by a kind gentleman who clearly understood horses. This gentleman took a great liking to me, and soon afterwards, he convinced my master to sell me to a friend of his, Mr. Barry, who wanted a safe, pleasant horse for riding. Mr. Barry was also kind to me, but because he could not keep me himself, he placed me in a hired stable. Here, unknown to Mr. Barry, I was not treated so well as I should have been. When he found out what was happening at the stables, he decided that as much as he liked me, he had to give up keeping a horse. Thus, I was sold again.

I was taken to a horse fair where I was put with two or three other strong, useful-looking horses, and a good many people came to look at us. The gentlemen always turned from me when they saw my broken knees. There was one man, I thought, if he would buy me, I should be happy. He was not a gentleman, nor yet one of the loud flashy sort that called themselves so. I knew in a moment, by the way he handled me, that he was used to horses; he spoke gently, and his grey eye had a kindly, cheery look in it. He offered twenty-three pounds for me; but that was refused, and he walked away. I looked after him, but he was gone, and a very hard-looking, loud-voiced man came. I was dreadfully afraid he would have me; but he walked off. Then the hard-faced man came back again and offered twenty-three pounds. A very close bargain was being driven; but just then the grey-eyed man came back again. I could not help reaching out my head towards him. He stroked my face kindly.

"Well, old chap," he said, "I think we should suit each other. I'll give twenty-four for him."

"Say twenty-five and you shall have him."

"Twenty-four ten," said my friend, in a very decided tone, "and not another sixpence—yes or no?"

"Done," said the salesman, "and you may depend upon it there's a monstrous deal of quality in that horse, and if you want him for cab work, he's a bargain."

My new master, a London cab driver, was Jeremiah Barker, but every one called him Jerry. Polly, his wife, was just as good a match as a man could have. She was a plump, trim, tidy little woman, with smooth dark hair, dark eyes, and a merry little mouth. He had a son, Harry, who was nearly twelve years old: a tall, frank, good-tempered lad; and little Dolly was her mother over again, at eight years old. They were all wonderfully fond of each other; I never knew such a happy, merry family before or since. Jerry had a cab of his own, and two horses, which he drove and attended to himself.

The next morning, when I was well groomed, Polly and Dolly came into the yard to see me and make friends. Harry had been helping his father since the early morning, and had stated his opinion that I should turn out a "regular brick." Polly brought me a slice of apple, and Dolly a piece of bread. It was a great treat to be petted again, and talked to in a gentle voice, and I let them see as well as I could that I wished to be friendly. Polly thought I was very handsome, and a great deal too good for a cab, if it was not for the broken knees.

"Of course there's no one to tell us whose fault that was," said Jerry, "and as long as I don't know, I shall give him the benefit of the doubt; for a firmer, neater stepper I never rode; we'll call him Jack, after the old one—shall we, Polly?"

"Do," she said, "for I like to keep a good name going."

Captain, Jerry's other horse, went out in the cab all morning. Harry came in after school to feed me and give me water. In the afternoon I was put into the cab. Jerry took as much pains to see if the collar and bridle fitted comfortably as if he had been John Manly over again. There was no bearing rein—no curb—nothing but a plain ring snaffle. What a blessing that was!

The first week of my life as a cab horse was very trying; I had never been used to London, and the noise, the hurry, the crowds of horses, carts, and carriages that I had to make my way through made me feel anxious and harassed; but I soon found that I could perfectly trust my driver, and then I made myself easy, and got used to it.

Jerry was as good a driver as I had ever known; and what was better, he took as much thought for his horses as he did for himself. He kept us very clean, and gave us as much change of food as he could, and always plenty of it; and not only that, but he always gave

us plenty of clean, fresh water, which he allowed to stand by us both night and day, except of course when we came in warm. But the best thing that we had here was our Sundays for rest; we worked so hard in the week that I do not think we could have kept up to it, but for that day.

The winter came in early, with a great deal of cold and wet. There was snow, or sleet, or rain, almost every day for weeks, changing only for keen driving winds, or sharp frosts. The horses all felt it very much. Some of the drivers had a waterproof cover to throw over them, which was a fine thing; but some of the men were so poor that they could not protect either themselves or their horses, and many of them suffered very much that winter. When we horses worked half the day we went to our dry stables, and could rest; whilst they had to sit on their boxes, sometimes staying out as late as one or two o'clock in the morning, if they had a party to wait for.

Christmas and the New Year are very merry times for some people; but for cabmen and cabmen's horses it is no holiday, though it may be a harvest. There are so many parties, balls, and places of amusement open, that the work is hard and often late. Sometimes driver and horse have to wait for hours in the rain or frost, shivering with cold, while the merry people within are dancing away to the music.

On the evening of the New Year, we took two gentlemen to a house in one of the West End squares. We set them down at nine o'clock and were told to come again at eleven. "But," said one of them, "you may have to wait a few minutes, but don't be late."

As the clock struck eleven we were at the door, for Jerry was always punctual. The clock chimed the quarters—one, two, three, and then struck twelve, but the door did not open.

The wind had been very changeable, with squalls of rain during the day, but now it came on a sharp driving sleet. Still the clock chimed the quarters, and no one came. At half-past twelve, he rang the bell and asked the servant if he would be wanted that night. "Oh!

yes, you'll be wanted safe enough," said the man, "you must not go, it will soon be over."

At a quarter past one the door opened, and the two gentlemen came out; they got into the cab without a word, and told Jerry where to drive, which was nearly two miles. When the men got out they never said they were sorry to have kept us waiting so long, but were angry at the charge: they had to pay for the two hours and a quarter waiting; but it was hard-earned money to Jerry.

At last we got home; he could hardly speak, and his cough was dreadful; he could hardly get his breath, but he gave me a rub down as usual, and even went up to the hayloft for an extra bundle of straw for my bed.

It was late the next morning before anyone came, and then it was only Harry. At noon he came again, and gave us our food and water: this time Dolly came with him; she was crying, and I could gather from what they said that Jerry was dangerously ill.

It was quickly settled that as soon as Jerry was well enough, they should remove to the country, and that the cab and horses should be sold as soon as possible.

The day came for going away. Jerry had not been allowed to go out yet, and I never saw him after that New Year's Eve. Polly and the children came to bid me good-bye. "Poor old Jack! dear old Jack! I wish we could take you with us," she said, and then, laying her hand on my mane, she put her face close to my neck and kissed me. Dolly was crying and kissed me too. Harry stroked me a great deal, but said nothing, only he seemed very sad, and so I was led away to my new place.

I was sold to a corn dealer and baker, whom Jerry knew, and with him he thought I should have good food and fair work. In the first he was quite right, and if my master had always been on the premises, I do not think I should have been overloaded, but there was a foreman who was always hurrying and driving every one, and frequently when I had quite a full load, he would order something else to be taken on. My carter's name was Jakes. Like the other carters, he always had the bearing rein up, which prevented me from drawing easily, and by the time I had been there three or four months, I found the work telling very much on my strength.

Good feed and fair rest will keep one's strength under full work, but no horse can stand against overloading; and I was getting so thoroughly pulled down from this cause, that a younger horse was bought in my place. However, I escaped without any permanent injury and was sold to a large cab owner.

I shall never forget my new master; he had black eyes, his mouth was as full of teeth as a bulldog's, and his voice was as harsh as the grinding of cart wheels over gravel stones. His name was Nicholas Skinner.

Skinner had a low set of cabs and a low set of drivers; he was hard on the men, and the men were hard on the horses. In this place we had no Sunday rest, and it was in the heat of summer. My life was

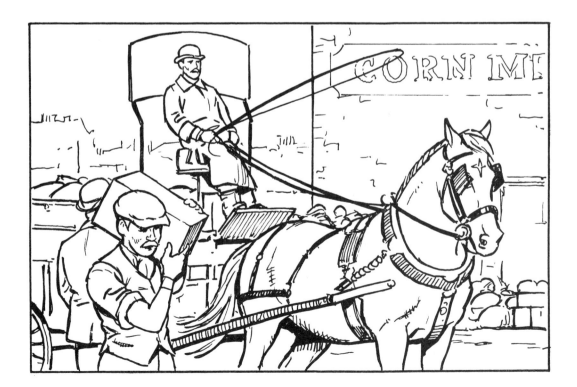

now so utterly wretched that I wished I might drop down dead at my work, and be out of my misery; and one day my wish nearly came to pass.

I went on the stand at eight in the morning, and had done a good share of work, when we had to take a fare to the railway. A long train was just expected in, and as all the cabs were soon engaged, ours was called for. There was a party of four; a noisy, blustering man with a lady, a little boy, and a young girl, and a great deal of luggage. The lady and the boy got into the cab, and while the man ordered about the luggage, the young girl came and looked at me.

"Papa," she said, "I am sure this poor horse cannot take us and all our luggage so far, he is so very weak and worn out. Do look at him."

"Nonsense, Grace, get in at once, and don't make all this fuss; there, get in and hold your tongue!"

My gentle friend had to obey; and box after box was dragged up and lodged on the top of the cab, or settled by the side of the driver. At last all was ready, and with his usual jerk at the rein, and slash of the whip, he drove out of the station.

I got along fairly till we came to Ludgate Hill, but there the heavy load and my own exhaustion were too much. I was struggling to keep on, when, in a single moment—I cannot tell how—my feet slipped from under me, and I fell heavily to the ground on my side; the suddenness and the force with which I fell seemed to beat all the breath out of my body. I heard a sort of confusion round me, loud, angry voices, and the getting down of the luggage, but it was all like a dream. I thought I heard that sweet, pitiful voice saying, "Oh! that poor horse! it is our fault." I cannot tell how long I lay there, but I found my life coming back, and a kind-voiced man was patting me and encouraging me to rise. After one or two attempts, I staggered to my feet, and was gently led to some stables which were close by.

The next morning, Skinner came with a farrier to look at me. He examined me closely and said: "This is a case of overwork more than disease. If he was broken-winded, you had better have him killed out of hand, but he is not; there is a sale of horses coming off in about ten days. If you rest him and feed him up, you may get more than his skin is worth, at any rate."

At this sale, I found myself in company with the old, broken-down

horses—some lame, some broken-winded, some old, and some that I am sure it would have been merciful to shoot.

The buyers and sellers too, looked not much better off than the poor beasts they were bargaining about. After some time, I noticed a man who looked like a gentleman farmer, with a young boy by his side. When he came up to me and my companions, he stood still, and gave a pitiful look round upon us. I saw his eye rest on me; I had still a good mane and tail, which did something for my appearance. I pricked my ears and looked at him.

"There's a horse, Willie, that has known better days." He put out his hand and gave me a kind pat on the neck. I put out my nose in answer to his kindness; the boy stroked my face.

"Poor old fellow! see, grandpa, how well he understands kindness."

The man who had brought me for sale now put in his word. "This 'ere hoss is just pulled down with overwork in the cabs; he's not an old one, and I heerd as how the vetenary should say, that a six months' run off would set him right up. I've had the tending of him these ten days past, and a gratefuller, pleasanter animal I never met with, and 'twould be worth a gentleman's while to give a five-pound note for him, and let him have a chance. I'll be bound he'd be worth twenty pounds next spring."

The farmer slowly felt my legs, which were much swelled and strained; then he looked at my mouth. "Thirteen or fourteen, I should say; just trot him out, will you?"

I arched my poor thin neck, raised my tail a little, and threw out my legs as well as I could, for they were very stiff.

" 'Tis a speculation," said the old gentleman, shaking his head, but at the same time slowly drawing out his purse—"quite a speculation! Have you any more business here?" he said, counting the sovereigns into the salesman's hand.

"No, sir, I can take him for you to the inn, if you please."

"Do so, I am now going there."

They walked forward, and I was led behind. The boy could hardly control his delight, and the old gentleman seemed to enjoy his pleasure. I had a good feed at the inn, and was then gently ridden home by a servant of my new master's and turned into a large meadow with a shed in one corner of it.

Mr. Thoroughgood, for that was the name of my benefactor, gave orders that I should have hay and oats every night and morning, and the run of the meadow during the day, and "you, Willie," said he, "must take the oversight of him; I give him in charge to you."

The boy was proud of his charge, and undertook it in all seriousness. There was not a day when he did not pay me a visit. He always came with kind words and caresses, and of course I grew very fond of him. He called me Old Crony. Sometimes he brought his grandfather, who always looked closely at my legs: "This is our point, Willie," he would say; "but he is improving so steadily that I think we shall see a change for the better."

The perfect rest, the good food, the soft turf, and gentle exercise soon began to tell on my condition and my spirits. During the winter my legs improved so much that I began to feel quite young again. The spring came round, and one day in March Mr. Thoroughgood determined that he would try me in the phaeton. I was well pleased,

and he and Willie drove me a few miles. My legs were not stiff now, and I did the work with perfect ease.

"He's growing young, Willie; we must give him a little gentle work now; he has a beautiful mouth, and good paces, they can't be better."

"Oh! grandpapa, how glad I am you bought him!"

"So am I, my boy, but he has to thank you more than me; we must now be looking out for a quiet, genteel place for him, where he will be valued."

One day during this summer the groom cleaned and dressed me with such extraordinary care that I thought some new change must be at hand. Willie seemed half anxious, half merry, as he got into the chaise with his grandfather.

"If the ladies take to him," said the old gentleman, "they'll be suited, and he'll be suited: we can but try."

A mile or two from the village, we came to a pretty, low house. Whilst Willie stayed with me, Mr. Thoroughgood went into the house. In about ten minutes he returned, followed by three ladies. They all came and looked at me and asked questions. The younger lady, Miss Ellen, took to me very much; she said she was sure she should like me, I had such a good face. It was then arranged that I should be sent for the next day.

In the morning a smart-looking young man came for me. I was led home, placed in a comfortable stable, fed and left to myself. The next day, when my groom was cleaning my face, he said: "That is just like the star that Black Beauty had, he is much the same height too; I wonder where he is now."

A little further on he came to the place in my neck where I was bled, and where a little knot was left in the skin. He almost started, and began to look me over carefully, talking to himself.

"White star in the forehead, one white foot on the off side, this little knot just in that place"—then looking at the middle of my back—"and as I am alive, there is that little patch of white hair that John used to call 'Beauty's three-penny bit.' It *must* be Black Beauty! Why, Beauty! Beauty! do you know me? little Joe Green that almost killed you?" He began patting and patting me as if he was quite overjoyed. I put my nose up to him, and tried to say that we were friends. I never saw a man so pleased.

"Give you a fair trial! I should think so indeed! I wonder who the rascal was that broke your knees, my old Beauty! You must have been badly served out somewhere; well, well, it won't be my fault if you haven't good times now. I wish John Manly was here to see you."

In the afternoon I was put into a low cart and brought to the door. Miss Ellen was going to try me, and Joe went with her. I soon found that she was a good driver, and she seemed pleased with my paces. I heard Joe telling her about me, and that he was sure I was Squire Gordon's old Black Beauty.

When we returned, Miss Ellen's sisters came out to hear how I had behaved myself. She told them what she had just heard, and said: "I shall certainly write to Mrs. Gordon, and tell her that her favourite horse has come to us. How pleased she will be!"

After this I was driven every day for a week or so, and as I

appeared to be quite safe, the ladies decided to keep me and call me by my old name of Black Beauty.

I have now lived in this happy place a whole year. Joe is the best and kindest of grooms. My work is easy and pleasant, and I feel my strength and spirits all coming back again. Mr. Thoroughgood said to Joe the other day: "In your place he will last till he is twenty years old—perhaps more."

Willie always speaks to me when he can, and treats me as his special friend. My ladies have promised that I shall never be sold, and so I have nothing to fear; and here my story ends. My troubles are all over, and I am at home; and often before I am quite awake, I fancy I am still in the orchard at Birtwick, standing with my old friends under the apple trees.